START YOUR ENGINES

5 -MINUTE STORIES

Houghton Mifflin Harcourt
Boston New York

CONTENTS

MARGRET & H.A.REY'S

Curious George Takes a Train

Illustrated in the style of H. A. Rey by Martha Weston

This is George.

He was a good little monkey and always very curious.

This morning George and the man with the yellow hat were at the train station.

They were taking a trip to the country with their friend,
Mrs. Needleman. But first they had to get tickets.

Inside the station everyone was in a hurry. People rushed
to buy newspapers to read and treats to eat. Then they
rushed to catch their trains.

But one little boy with a brand-new toy engine was not in a hurry. Nor was the small crowd next to him. They were just standing in one spot looking up. George looked up, too.

A trainmaster was moving numbers and letters on a big sign.

Soon the trainmaster was called away. But his job did not look finished. George was curious. Could he help?

George climbed up in a flash.

Then, just like the trainmaster, he picked a letter off the sign and put it in a different place.

Next he took the number 9 and put it near a 2.

George moved more letters and more numbers.

He was glad to be such a big help.

ARRIVALS				DEPARTURES			
CITY	TIME		TRACK	CITY	TIME		TRACK
NEW CITY	6:30 AM		8	OVERDALE	6:15 AM		2
HILLTOP	7:00 AM		3	SMALLBURG	7:25 AM		7
OVERDALE	7:15 AM		4	NEW CITY	7:50 AM		6
SMALLBURG	7:45 AM			CITY	8:08 AM		3
BIG CITY	8:00 AM			DLETON	8:15 AM		5
MIDDLETON	8:02 AM		1	OWNSVILLE	8:40 AM		2
OLD TOWN	A:45 AM		2	HILLTOP	9:25 AM		1
TOWNSVILLE	9:10 AM		5	OLD TOWN	9:55 AM		8

"Hey," yelled a man from below. "I can't tell when my train leaves!"

"What track is my train on?" asked another man.

"What's that monkey doing up there?" demanded a woman. She did not sound happy.

The trainmaster did not
sound happy either: "Come
down from there right now!"
he hollered at George.

Poor George. It's too easy for a monkey to get into trouble. But, lucky for George, it's also easy for a monkey to get out of trouble.

Right then the conductor shouted, "All aboard!"

A crowd of people rushed toward the train. George simply slid down a pole, scurried over a suitcase, and squeezed with the crowd through the gate. There he found the perfect hiding place for a monkey.

The little boy with the toy engine also
ran through the gate.

"Look, Daddy," he said, "a train!"

His father looked up. "Come back,
son," he yelled. "That's not our train!"

But it was too late. The gate locked behind him.
The boy began to cry.
George peeked out of his hiding place.
He saw the boy's toy roll toward the tracks.
The boy ran after it.

This time George knew he could help.
He leaped out of his hiding place and ran
fast. George grabbed the toy engine before
the little boy came too close to the tracks.

What a close call!

When the trainmaster opened the gate, the
boy's father ran to his son.

The boy was not crying now.

He was playing with his new friend.

"So, there you are," said the trainmaster when he saw George.
"You sure made a lot of trouble on the big board!"

"Please don't be upset with him," said the boy's father.
"He saved my son."

The people on the platform agreed.
They had seen what had happened,
and they clapped and cheered.
George was a hero!

Just then the man with the yellow hat arrived with
Mrs. Needleman. "It's time to go, George," he said.
"Here comes our train."

"This is our train, too," the father said. The little
boy was excited. "Can George ride with us?" he asked.

That sounded like a good idea to everyone. So the
trainmaster asked the conductor to find them a special
seat.

And he did.
Right up front.

The end.

A JOKE FROM
Little Blue Truck

What do you tell
a little pickup who's
feeling blue?

Keep on trucking!

NANCY COFFELT

Pug in a Truck

For Dutch, Maggie, Chip, Belle, Fred, Judy, Pooh, Chloe, and Ollie,
our four-legged family members.

This is our truck.
It's flat in the front.

This is me.
My nose is as
flat as the front
of our truck.

This is my friend.
He calls me Pug.
I'm Pug in a truck!

This is where we pick up
our load to deliver.
When we hook up the trailer,
our truck's not a bobtail anymore.
Sometimes we haul goods for
stores to sell. Sometimes we
haul food that farmers
have grown.

Sniff, sniff.

No food in this cargo!

My friend lifts me into the cab.

RUMBLE, RUMBLE.

The diesel engine growls.

GRUMBLE, GRUMBLE.

So do I.

Bow-wow!

We have a load
to deliver!

We get on the
freeway and put
the hammer down.

Now we're heading straight out of the city.

We see lots of other
vehicles on the road. Look—

a dragon wagon, a roller skate,

a four-wheeler, and a skateboard!

But I'm always on the lookout for
big rigs like ours.

Finally, I see an eighteen-wheeler hauling a load of toothpicks.

Look at me! I'm as tough as your truck.
HONK - HONK
goes the driver.
Bow-wow,
I'm as loud as
your horn!

Badadadada!

Our air brakes bark.

Bow-wow!

So do I.

Ground clouds —
my friend can't see the road!

We switch on our fog lights.
"Pug, only five more yardsticks until we're over
the pass and in the clear."

Bow-wow, everybody follow us!
Our fog lights lead the way.
So do my barks.

Bow-wow — one mile!
Bow-wow — two miles!
Three, four, five — we made it!

Crackle goes the CB.

"You got your ears on? Thanks, barking buddy. You helped everyone keep the shiny side up and the greasy side down."

Bow-wow, that's my job!

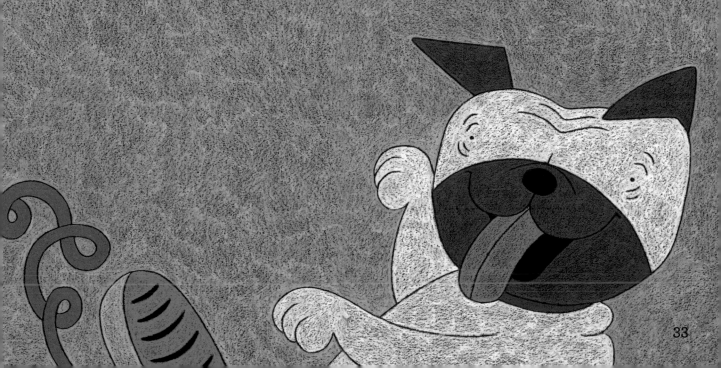

Now we're at double nickel again and back in business. But all that barking has

tired

me

out.

Bow-wow,
truck stop!

We can fuel up here.

Our truck needs diesel, but I eat dog food.

My friend needs to fuel up too.
But no pugs allowed in the restaurant.

After dinner we take a walk around the truck stop.

There drivers can get their hair cut or their shoes shined. They can buy snacks or maps.

And some drivers are here to park their trucks and get some sleep. **Bow-wow,** it's our bedtime too.

This is our bed,
behind the cab.

It's soft and warm
and we need to rest.

Because tomorrow we're back on the road.

I'm Pug in a truck, and we have a load to deliver!

Trucker Glossary

Bobtail
a truck running without a trailer.

Double nickel
fifty-five miles per hour, the speed limit.

Dragon wagon
a tow truck.

Eighteen-wheeler
any articulated truck (even though many have fewer or more than eighteen wheels).

Four-wheeler
a passenger car.

Got your ears on?
an expression used when looking for someone on the CB. ("Hey, HT, you got your ears on?")

Ground clouds
fog.

Hammer down
to go fast, step on it.

Keeping the shiny side up and the greasy side down
driving safely, avoiding an accident.

Roller skate
any small car. Originally referred to a Volkswagen.

Skateboard
a flatbed trailer.

Toothpicks
a load of lumber.

Yardstick
a mile marker alongside a highway.

A JOKE FROM
Little Blue Truck

What does a city street
eat for breakfast?

Traffic jam!

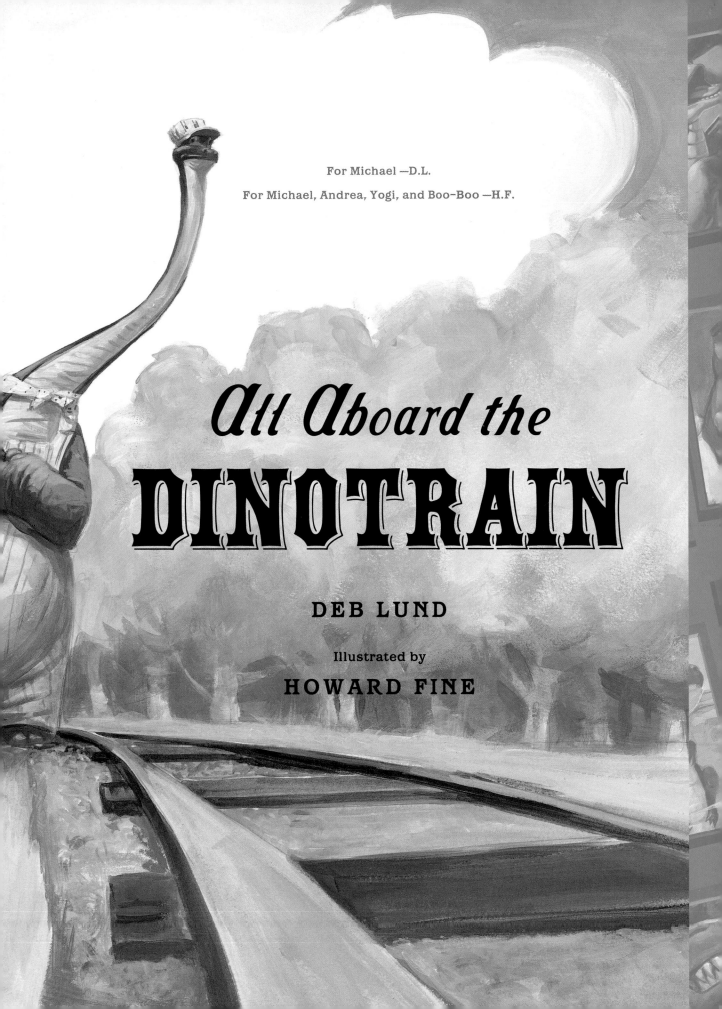

For Michael —D.L.

For Michael, Andrea, Yogi, and Boo-Boo —H.F.

All Aboard the

DINOTRAIN

DEB LUND

Illustrated by

HOWARD FINE

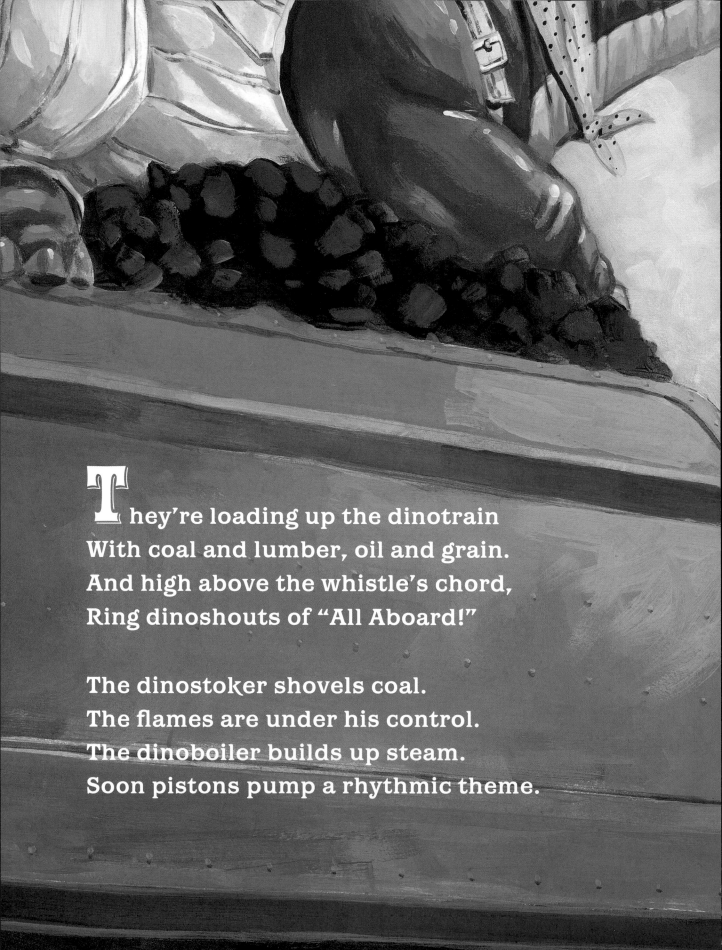

They're loading up the dinotrain
With coal and lumber, oil and grain.
And high above the whistle's chord,
Ring dinoshouts of "All Aboard!"

The dinostoker shovels coal.
The flames are under his control.
The dinoboiler builds up steam.
Soon pistons pump a rhythmic theme.

"Farewell!" the dinofamilies cry.
With cheers, the dinos wave good-bye.
Adventures wait just down the track.
"We're off!" they say. "But we'll be back!"

The engine coughs and dinochugs.
The train moves like a line of slugs.
"We haven't traveled very far.
Let's dinopush each railroad car!"

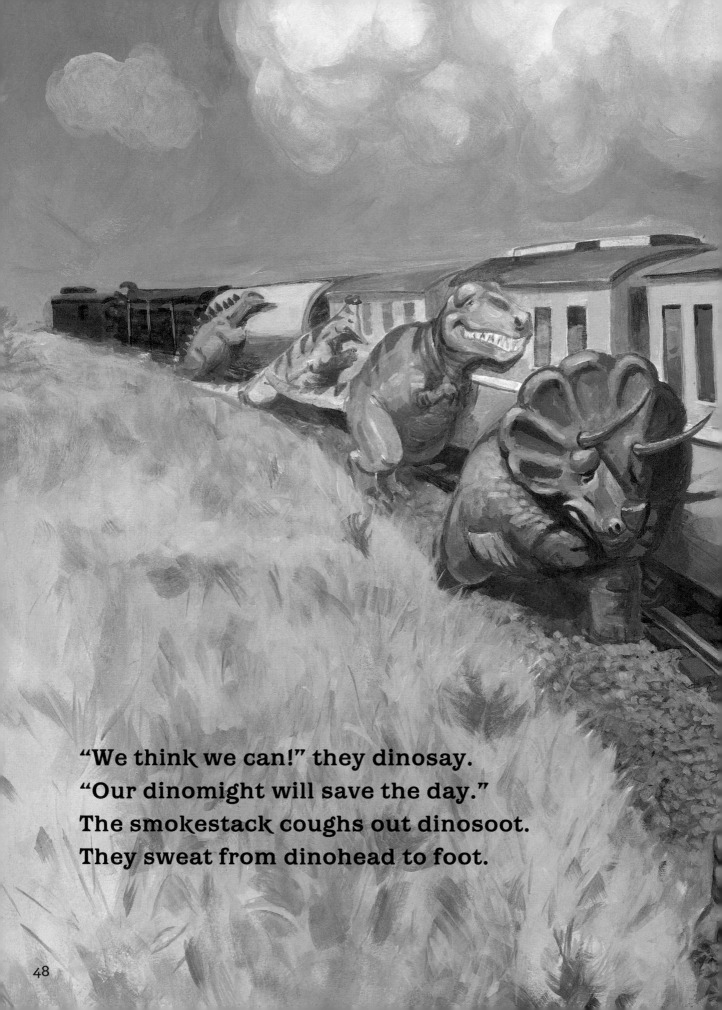

"We think we can!" they dinosay.
"Our dinomight will save the day."
The smokestack coughs out dinosoot.
They sweat from dinohead to foot.

The hill's too steep for that much weight,
And so they toss the dinofreight.
Without a load, they quickly climb
And reach the peak in dinotime.

A dark and narrow dinotunnel
Sucks and spits them through its funnel.
Out the chute and down the slide,
A roller-coaster dinoride!

They dinoscream and squeal, "Yippee!"
And wave their dinoarms with glee.
When the cars tip left or right,
They lean way out and hang on tight.

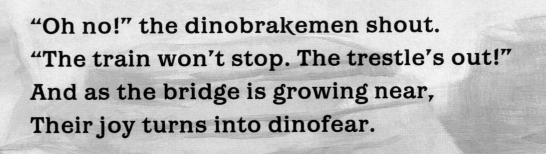

"Oh no!" the dinobrakemen shout.
"The train won't stop. The trestle's out!"
And as the bridge is growing near,
Their joy turns into dinofear.

They clamber up and cling on top,
Unsure of how they'll dinostop.
They dinoduck and hide their eyes,
But then they get a *big* surprise.

They dinorocket off the bridge,
While train cars fly from ridge to ridge.
The train goes on without a crash.
"We're dinoflying!" Then . . .

They dinogroan, "How can it be?
We thought this trip was water-free!
What made us want to dinoroam?
Let's shake this lake and head back home!"

They pile aboard a handcar there
To seesaw back with dinoflair.
They dinopump instead of chug
And make it home for one big hug.

Though dinotight in that embrace,
They still find dinodreams to chase.
"We'll never take another train . . .

But how about a dinoplane?"

A JOKE FROM
Little Blue Truck

What do you call Little Blue
when he gives a cow a ride?

Moo!

A moo-ving van.

Farmer Dale's Red Pickup Truck

WRITTEN BY LISA WHEELER

ILLUSTRATED BY IVAN BATES

In memory of my mother,
Barbara Budai Haroulakis,
who always made room, in her heart
and her home, for more.
—L.W.

To Lorna, Martin, Jonah, and Leo.
—I.B.

Farmer Dale's red pickup truck
hauled a load of hay.
A bossy cow, with eyes of brown,
was standing in the way.

"How 'bout a ride?" asked Bossy Cow.

"Hop in," said Farmer Dale.

"Mooove over!" ordered Bossy Cow.

"There's no room for my tail."

The truck bounced up. The truck bounced down.
It spit and sputtered toward the town.

Farmer Dale's red pickup truck
was chugging right along.
A woolly sheep came strolling by,
bleating out a song.

"Room for more?" sang Woolly Sheep.
"Fit me in somehow?"
"No problem," answered Farmer Dale.
"Mooove over!" uttered Cow.

The truck bounced up and shimmied.
It coughed and wheezed back down.
The pickup spit a cloud of smoke
and sputtered toward the town.

Farmer Dale's red pickup truck
hit a rocky bump.
It swerved beside a roly pig,
skating past the dump.
"Oh, my stars!" squealed Roly Pig.
"You folks just knocked me down."
"So sorry," Dale apologized.
"Need a ride to town?"

"I do indeed," said Roly Pig.
"My skates are broken now."
"Climb aboard," sang Woolly Sheep.
"Mooove over!" ordered Cow.

The truck bounced up and groaned back down.
It hiccuped twice and chugged toward town.

Farmer Dale's red pickup truck
slowly rattled on.
A goat with an accordion
stood grazing on the lawn.
"Can I squeeze in?" asked Nanny Goat.
"My pleasure," Farmer said.

"Ba-a-a-d idea," sang Woolly Sheep.
"The engine's almost dead."
"No room!" lamented Roly Pig.
"We're overcrowded now!"
"We'll make some room," said Farmer Dale.
"Mooove over!" bossed the cow.

The truck bounced up. The springs all popped.
The bumper bumped. The pickup stopped.

Farmer Dale's red pickup truck
stood stranded in the road.
"It seems you have a problem,"
a cocky rooster crowed.
"We do," admitted Farmer Dale.
"The problem is we're stuck.
The weight of all these animals
is too much for my truck."
Rooster eyed the animals.
"You're such a cozy group.
I hate to cluck like Mother Hen,
but who will fly the coop?"

"I just squeezed in," said Nanny Goat.

"I'm faint," squealed Roly Pig.

"I won't mooove," said Bossy Cow.

"I'm boss of this red rig."

"Too ba-a-a-d for you," sang Woolly Sheep.

"The biggest has to go."

"Settle down," said Farmer Dale.

"Let's think now—nice and slow."

"I'll get out," the farmer said,
"and push us from the rear."
"Good idea," said Nanny Goat.
Cow replied, "I'll steer."
Farmer Dale's red pickup truck
didn't budge at all.
Dale pushed until his face was red,
and then he heard a call.

"Can I butt in?" asked Nanny Goat.
"I'd like to lend a hoof."
Rooster squawked, "I'll point the way,"
then roosted on the roof.

"I'll pitch in," sang Woolly Sheep.
"I'll ra-a-a-m it with my head."
"Don't hog the fun," said Roly Pig.
"Let's all help out, instead."

The pickup rocked and rumbled.
It rolled an inch or so.
"It's moooving!" shouted Bossy Cow.
The rooster crowed, "Too slow!"
"Turn the key," said Farmer Dale.
"I can't!" the cow replied.
"She's got no ha-a-a-nds,"
  explained the sheep.
  Farmer Dale just sighed.

"You should steer," said Bossy Cow.
"We'll mooove this heap along."
The beasts all pushed together
and sang a working song.

The pickup bounced and shimmied.
It groaned and squeaked and wheezed.
It spit a thankful cloud of smoke
and started with a sneeze.

Farmer Dale's red pickup truck
rumbled into town,
hauling Goat and Pig and Sheep,
and Cow with eyes of brown.
Rooster roosting on the hood
cried, "Cock-a-doodle-cluck!"

"Hip-hooray for Farmer Dale
and his red pickup truck!"

A JOKE FROM
Little Blue Truck

What is Little Blue Truck's
favorite dance move?

Brake dancing.

MONSTER TRUCKS!

HVYDTY

MARK TODD

Monster trucks!
Monster trucks!
Giant dirt-dumping trucks.
Heaving and hauling
heavy loads of rubble,
tipping his load
without any trouble.

Monster trucks!
Monster trucks!
Green gargling garbage trucks.
Eating and crunching,
munching and slurping.
Just don't be around
when this guy starts burping.

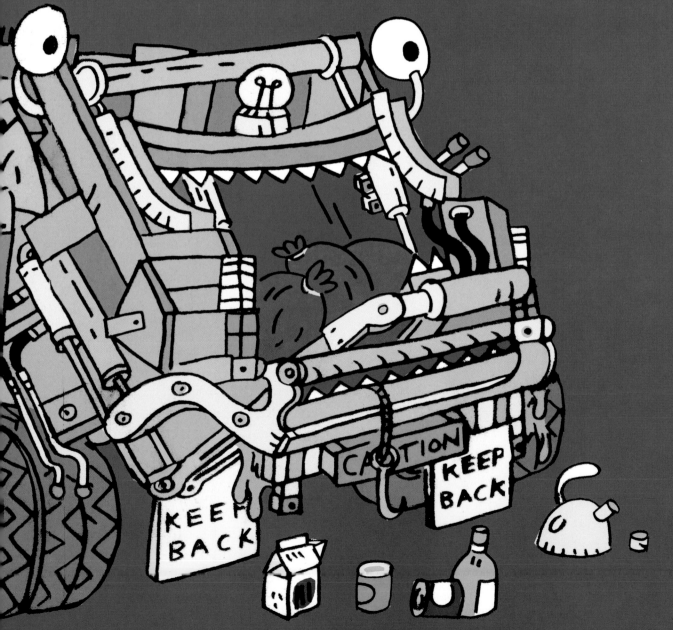

Monster trucks!
Monster trucks!
Sloshing steel tanker trucks.
A milk-hungry heifer,
a big-bellied beast—
a vitamin-D dose
for strong bones and teeth.

Monster trucks!
Monster trucks!
Big bulldozer trucks.
Scraping and shoveling
with a sneering tooth blade,
leveling the earth
for the roads to be laid.

Monster trucks!
Monster trucks!
Smooth steamroller trucks.
He'll squash and crush
and flatten out
anything that comes
under his powerful snout.

Monster trucks!
Monster trucks!
Flame-fighting fire trucks.
Sirens wailing and blaring,
lights blazing and whirring—
rushing off to put out
whatever is burning.

Monster trucks!
Monster trucks!
Rolling round mixer trucks.
Belly churning and turning,
jumbling and tumbling.
For all that he eats
you think it'd stop grumbling.

Monster trucks!
Monster trucks!
Eighteen-wheel semi trucks.
Stacks huffing and puffing,
engine creating a roar.
From coast to coast,
that's a big 10-4.

Monster trucks!
Monster trucks!
Heavy-duty digging trucks.
Using a steely clawed arm,
with a thirty-foot reach,
what a great shoveling partner
to have at the beach.

Monster trucks!
Monster trucks!
Mighty, massive MONSTER trucks!
They squash and crush,
churn and crunch,
pack and stack
and mix and munch!

CHUCK

DUMP TRUCK

Weight 105 tons, empty; 275 tons, full

Top speed 34 miles per hour (7 miles per hour in reverse)

Tires 9 1/2 feet tall

Special feature Hydraulic pumps can lift and dump a load in 15 seconds.

STINK

GARBAGE TRUCK

Weight 17 tons, empty

Capacity Up to 20 cubic yards of trash

Special feature Hydraulic compacting jaw can crush a couch in seconds.

SEÑOR MOO

MILK TANKER TRUCK

Length 67 feet

Weight 15 tons, empty; 35 tons, full

Capacity 40,000 pounds of milk

Tank Stainless steel, sterile, and refrigerated to below 40°F during storage and transportation.

Special feature Milk is pumped into the storage tank at 1,200 to 1,500 pounds per minute. Suction hoses unload the tank in less than 15 minutes.

DOZER

BULLDOZER

Weight 42 tons

Blade 14 feet wide

Special feature Heavy-duty blade has reinforced steel cutting teeth for easy tearing.

SMOOSH

ROLLER TRUCK

Weight 17 tons

Roller width 84 inches

Compaction pressure 26,550 pounds per square inch

Special feature Water spray system keeps rollers cool on hot asphalt.

BIG RED
FIRE TRUCK (LADDER TRUCK)

Length 40 feet

Weight 22 tons

Ladder reach Up to 100 feet

Top speed 75 miles per hour

Special feature Carries 800 feet of hose, which can pump up to 1,500 gallons of water per minute.

MISH-MASH
CONCRETE MIXER

Weight 18 tons, empty

Capacity 12 cubic yards

Chute 10 feet long and can be rotated in order to guide cement

Special feature Barrel spins one way to mix the cement and spins the other way to pour.

LONG JOHN
SEMITRAILER TRUCK

Length Up to 80 feet

Weight 18 tons, empty; up to 40 tons, full

Capacity 35,000 cubic feet

Special features 18 wheels and a sleeper compartment with bunk beds and television. A driver may travel more than 175,000 miles a year.

DOUG
DIGGER OR EXCAVATOR

Height 15 feet to top of cab

Length of arm 38 feet

Weight 104 tons

Special feature Hydraulic arm can reach up to 44 feet high and dig 28 feet down.

A JOKE FROM
Little Blue Truck

Why did Little Blue Truck
stop driving?

He got tired.

Sheep in a Jeep

Nancy Shaw

Illustrated by
Margot Apple

To Allison and Danny —N.S.   To Sue Sherman —M.A.

Beep! Beep!
Sheep in a jeep
on a hill that's
steep.

Uh-oh!
The jeep won't go.

Sheep leap
to push the jeep.

Sheep shove.
Sheep grunt.
Sheep don't think
to look up front.

Jeep goes splash!
Jeep goes thud!

Jeep goes deep
in gooey mud.

Sheep shrug.

Sheep tug.

Sheep yelp.

Sheep get help.

Jeep comes out.

Sheep shout.

Sheep cheer.

Oh, dear!
   The driver sheep
      forgets to steer.

Jeep in a heap.

Sheep weep.

Sheep sweep the heap.

Jeep for sale — cheap.

A JOKE FROM
Little Blue Truck

How did the crow contact Little Blue Truck?

He made a long-distance caw.

RUSH HOUR

Christine Loomis • Illustrated by Mari Takabayashi

For Hutch, whose love and enthusiasm for things with wheels is awesome —C.L

For my mother in Tokyo and for the memory of my father —M.T.

Alarms are buzzing,
Day is dawning,

Sleepy people
Wake up yawning.

Showers splash,
Teeth are brushed,

Hair is combed,
Breakfast rushed.

Out their doors
Go moms and dads,
Lugging tools
Or books and pads.

Some alone,
Some with strollers,
Walkers, runners,
Readers, rollers,

Running,
Jumping
Onto trains,

subways,

Buses,

boats,

and planes,

Taxis,

bikes,

a car-pool van,

Cars of blue and
red and tan.

Engines start up with a jerk.
People hurry off to work.

Horns go beep-beep,
Whistles blow,

Planes go fast,
Trucks go slow.

Trolleys sway,
Ferries rock,

Time keeps ticking
On the clock.

Cars on side streets,
Trains on tracks,
Whizzing,
Zipping,
Clicky
Clack,

Rumbling,
Roaring,
Jiggling,
Jumping,
Left turn,
Right turn,
Backing,
Bumping.

Through the tunnels,
On the highways,

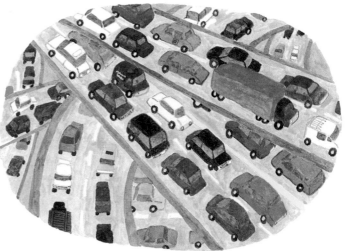

Over bridges,
Roads, and byways,

Down the river,

In the air,

People rushing everywhere!

In a blink
They disappear.
Trains are empty,

Tunnels clear.

Streets are quiet,
No more mobs.

People have begun
their jobs.

When day is over,
Each job ends.

Workers wave
Good-bye to
friends.

147

Then they race
To catch the trains,

Subways,

buses,

Boats,

and planes,

Taxis,

bikes,

A car-pool van,

Cars of blue and red and tan.

Down the river,
Underground,
Traffic creeping
Homeward bound.

Over bridges,
Roads, and byways,
Through the tunnels,
On the highways,

Right turn,
Left turn,
Backing,
Bumping,
Roaring,
Rumbling,
Jiggling,
Jumping,
Whizzing,
Zipping,
Clicky
Clack,
Cars on side
    streets,
  Trains on tracks.

Horns go beep-beep,

Whistles blow.

Nighttime lights

Begin to glow.

Doors swing open.
Kids run fast.

Moms and dads
Are home at last.

A JOKE FROM
Little Blue Truck

Why did Little Blue Truck
drive to the river when
he ran out of money?

Because it has a bank.

Here Comes Darrell

Leda Schubert

ILLUSTRATED BY

Mary Azarian

In memory of Darrell K. Farnham,
1936–2002

To Bob, and with immense gratitude to Mary
Azarian and Ann Rider —L.S.

In memory of master carpenter Luke Hardy,
my "Darrell" —M.A.

T he thermometer reads two below zero and it's snowing hard at four a.m., but Darrell is ready to work.

"I'll be home for breakfast," he says to Judy.
"I'll make eggs and home fries," she promises.

The main roads will be cleared by the town snowplows, but people with long driveways will be trapped without Darrell. His old truck starts on the second try and Buster jumps into the front seat. It's so cold that Darrell's nose hairs freeze. As he pulls away, he notices his barn roof sagging under the weight of the snow.

First Darrell plows out folks who must get to work early. Porch lights flash in thanks, and he blinks his headlights back. His stomach growls as he glimpses a neighbor making breakfast.

By seven a.m. he has plowed twenty-one driveways.

The truck radio blares, "All local schools are closed."

"Good thing. Right, Buster?" Buster barks. The roads are too slippery for schoolbuses.

The Harts' driveway is so steep and narrow that there's not much room to dump the heavy snow. As Darrell lowers the plow, the rear wheels slide off the road. He rocks the truck back and forth, back and forth. The tires swirl, the engine whines, and the back end swings closer to a ditch.

"Come on, come on." Darrell thumps the dashboard . . .

. . . and the truck jumps forward. Buster almost falls off the seat.

At the house, Tommy Hart waves. "Mom says come have coffee."

"Tell her thanks, but I've got lots more driveways."

"Can I help?"

"For a minute." Tommy climbs onto Darrell's lap and they plow a hill of snow.

"Oh boy! Mom and I can go sledding!" Tommy jumps down.

"She'll like that." Darrell says. He turns toward his twenty-third driveway and begins to think about Judy's fried eggs.

It's forty degrees when Darrell finishes loading his dump truck on a spring morning. Winter weather hangs on forever in northern Vermont, and the air still smells like wood smoke.

Since dawn Darrell has been splitting logs. The Barretts had run out of firewood and called him in a panic.

"We don't know when we'll be able to pay you," said Mr. Barrett.

"That's okay," Darrell said. "Keep those kids warm."

Just before Darrell leaves, Judy calls, "Don't forget about our barn roof. Looks like a good wind will lift it right off."

Darrell picks up Buster. "I'll get to it soon," he says.

Mud season has arrived, and the dirt roads are like chocolate pudding. The truck hits a rut and shoots sideways, sinking into a hole at the bottom of the Barretts' hill. Darrell and Buster wade through the mud up to the house.

"Looks like I'm stuck," he tells them.

"We're coming," says Mrs. Barrett. The Barretts and their two kids, David and Beth, help Darrell unload the wood.

"I'll be back for the truck," Darrell says. That evening, when the ruts freeze, Judy will bring him over on the tractor and they'll pull the truck out.

"We'll drive you home," Mrs. Barrett offers. "But come in first for some apple pie."

"No time. But I almost forgot these." He hands carefully carved birds to David and Beth.

"Will you teach me to whittle?" Beth asks.

"Sure." When his own kids were little, Darrell taught them to whittle, too.

Beth grins. "Then I'm going to learn to carve a dog just like Buster."

It's eighty-five degrees and the black flies are biting when Darrell starts his backhoe. The Murphys are building a new room, and Darrell is the excavator.

Judy reminds him about the barn. "Winter will be here sooner than we think."

"It doesn't look that bad," Darrell says, but it does.

The backhoe is a large machine, but Darrell is an artist. If a hammer drops on the ground, he can pick it up with the big bucket as if he's using tweezers.

He begins scooping and moves load after load of earth.

The Murphys arrive as he finishes digging. Andy Murphy throws a ball for Buster and it flies into the hole. Buster jumps in after it and can't climb out.

"Sorry!" Andy cries.

"Don't worry, Andy." Darrell swings the bucket around, gently picks up Buster, and deposits him on the bank. Buster shakes off.

"You folks interested in a pond over there?" Darrell asks. He points down the hill. "It'll be great for frogs and birds."

"I want frogs," Andy says, and his parents nod yes.

The Murphys hear the backhoe for the rest of the day, and the next, and the next. Every day Andy brings his frog net and watches the pond fill with water.

It's fifty degrees and the wind is fierce when Darrell, Judy, and Buster climb into the old truck on a brilliant October day. They are off to visit neighbors to see what everybody needs before winter. Judy keeps a list.

"What about our barn?" she asks.

"Tomorrow. I promise," Darrell says. And he means it, because soon the cows will have to come inside.

Some people need to have their driveways fixed. Some need firewood. The wind picks up and the list grows longer. Tree branches crash onto the road, and Darrell holds tight to the steering wheel on a gusty hill.

"Now *I'm* worried about that roof," he says.

When they get home, their barn roof is gone.

Darrell slams on the brakes and jumps out of the truck. Buster runs in wild circles. They hurry to the barn, where the Harts and Barretts are already taking measurements.

Mr. Murphy greets Darrell. "We saw it go and rushed right over," he explains.

"We're going to have a roof raising!" says Beth Barrett.

Darrell looks so embarrassed that Mr. Murphy says, "You've helped all of us over and over. We're happy to help you."

Mrs. Hart leads Darrell to the table. "We brought over some supper. Come and eat."

It is getting dark outside, but inside it feels as if the sun is shining. Beth Barrett, Andy Murphy, and Tommy Hart bring Darrell and Judy heaping plates of stew and pie, and everybody is safe and sound, even Darrell.

A JOKE FROM
Little Blue Truck

Why does Little Blue Truck
look like he's crying when it rains?

Because he uses his windshield weepers.

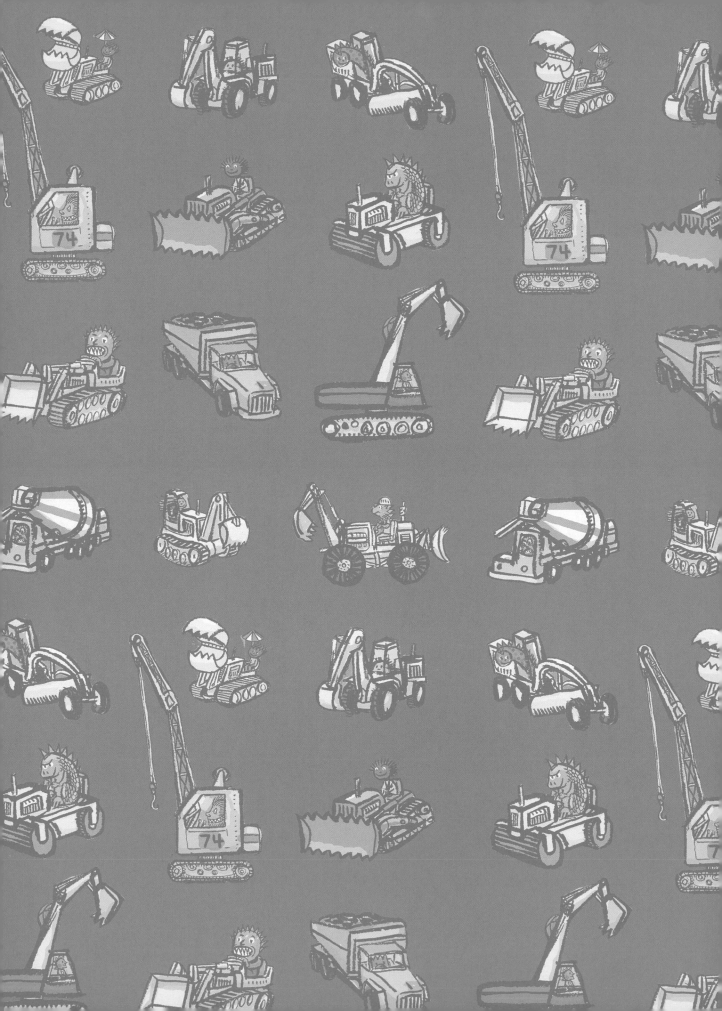

DIRTY
DUGG

GORBERT

MONSTERS
ON MACHINES

DEB LUND

Illustrated by
ROBERT NEUBECKER

For our own little monster,
Jean Michael —D.L.

For my besties, Izzy and Jo —R.N.

STINKY
STUBB

MELVINA

Construction crew monsters arrive on the scene.
They don hard hats before they go near a machine.

Leather work gloves,
some earplugs,
and big, heavy boots
are required for safety
by all builder brutes.

Stinky Stubb's the mechanic. He checks out the grader, the tractor, the cranes, and the big monster-vater.

Once engines are greased and the gears start to spin, he shrieks to the others that work can begin.

Foreman Gorbert stomps over. He's huge and he's hairy.
He grunts out the orders and adds, "Make it scary!"

The site's almost ready. The blueprints are drawn.
It's a Custom Prehaunted with thistles for lawn.

Flinging dirt like tornadoes, they holler and hoot.
(Monsters love getting grimy from hard hat to boot.)

They're transformed by the tractor, the crawler, the paver.
But bulldozers bring out *true* monster behavior.

They take turns on the steamroller, forklift, and crane,
till construction and cleanup are all that remain.

The cement trucks arrive. The foundation is poured.
Then they carefully place every brick, every board.

When the building is up and they gaze at the sight,
they can hardly contain their disgusting delight.
"How enchanting!" "How spooky!" "How frightfully fine!"
"The colors all clash. The design is divine!"

Once the landscaping, sidewalks, and roads are complete,
it's time to clean up so all's tidy and neat.
Without too much whining, they each do their share.
Melvina, Stubb, Gorbert, and Dugg know what's fair.

So clear out of the way if you see them around—
they're an organized earthquake reshaping the ground.
These builders are proud of the job that they do . . .

. . . on their mud-mounding,
nail-pounding,
monsterous crew.

A JOKE FROM
Little Blue Truck

Why did the cow
cross the road?

To get to the udder side.

KATY
AND THE
BIG SNOW

STORY AND PICTURES
BY
VIRGINIA LEE BURTON

HOUGHTON MIFFLIN COMPANY BOSTON

For Johnny from Jinnee

Katy was a beautiful red crawler tractor.
She was very big and very strong
and she could do a lot of things.

Katy had a bulldozer
to push dirt around with.

Katy also had a snow plow
to plow snow with.

Katy belonged to the Highway Department
of the City of Geoppolis.

The Highway Department repaired the roads in the summer
and kept them clear of snow in the winter
so traffic could run in and out and around the city.

All summer Katy worked on the roads
with her bulldozer.
Katy liked to work.
The harder and tougher the job
the better she liked it.

Once when the steamroller fell in the pond
Katy pulled it out.
The Highway Department was very proud of her.
They used to say, "Nothing can stop her."

When winter came
they put snow plows
on the big trucks
and changed Katy's bulldozer
for her snow plow.

But Katy was so big and strong
she had to stay at home,
because there was not enough snow for her to plow.

Then early one morning it started to drizzle.
The drizzle turned into rain.
The rain turned into snow.
By noon it was four inches deep.
The Highway Department sent out the truck plows.

By afternoon the snow was ten inches deep
and still coming down.
"Looks like a Big Snow,"
they said at the Highway Department,
and sent Katy out.

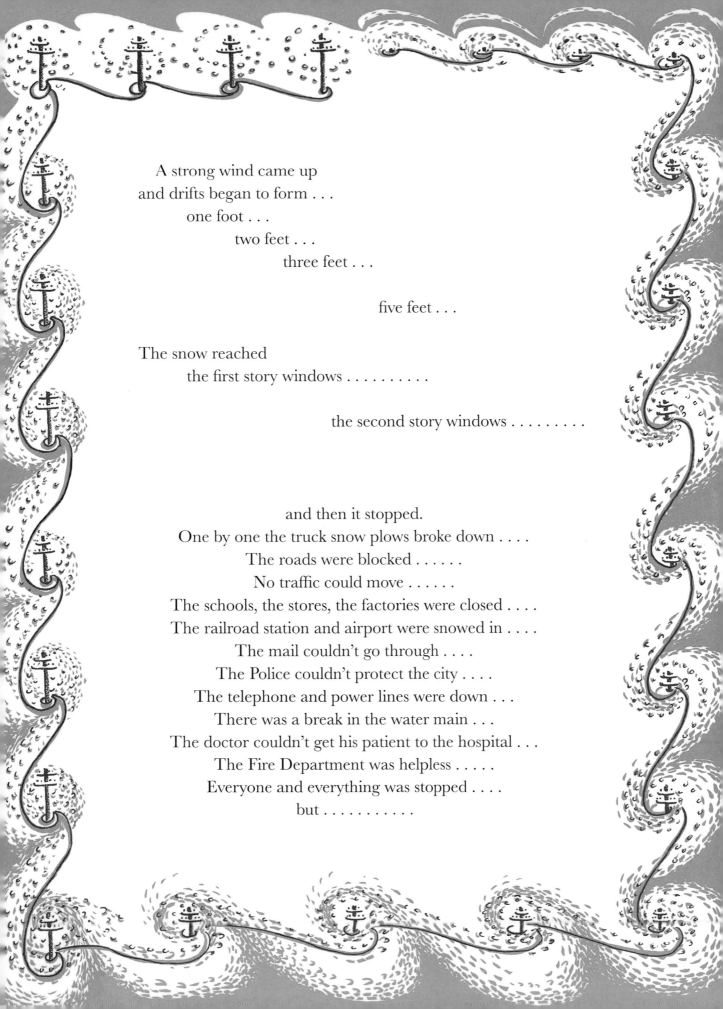

A strong wind came up
and drifts began to form . . .
one foot . . .
two feet . . .
three feet . . .

five feet . . .

The snow reached
the first story windows . . . .

the second story windows . . . .

and then it stopped.
One by one the truck snow plows broke down . . . .
The roads were blocked . . . . . .
No traffic could move . . . . . .
The schools, the stores, the factories were closed . . . .
The railroad station and airport were snowed in . . . .
The mail couldn't go through . . . .
The Police couldn't protect the city . . . .
The telephone and power lines were down . . .
There was a break in the water main . . .
The doctor couldn't get his patient to the hospital . . .
The Fire Department was helpless . . . . .
Everyone and everything was stopped . . . .
but . . . .

KATY

The City of Geoppolis was covered
with a thick blanket of snow.

Slowly and steadily
Katy started to plow out the city.

"Help!" called the Chief of Police.
"Help us to get out to protect the city."
"Sure," said Katy. "Follow me."

So Katy plowed out the center of the city.

"Help," called out the Postmaster.
"Help us get the mail through."
"Sure," said Katy. "Follow me."

So Katy plowed down to the Railway Station.

"Help! Help!" called out the Telephone Company
and the Electric Company.
"The poles are down somewhere in East Geoppolis."
"Follow me," said Katy.

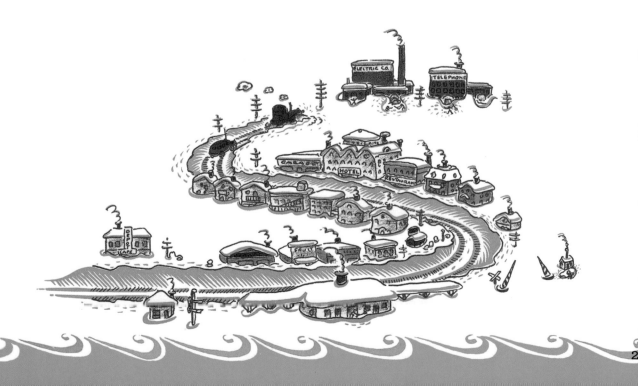

So Katy plowed out the roads to East Geoppolis.

"Help!"
called out the Superintendent of the Water Department.
"There's a break in the water main
somewhere in North Geoppolis."
"Follow me," said Katy

and she plowed out the roads to
North Geoppolis.

"Help! Emergency!" called out the doctor.
"Help me get this patient to the hospital
way out in West Geoppolis."
"Sure," said Katy. "Follow me."

So Katy plowed out the roads to the hospital.

"Help! Help! Help!" called out the Fire Chief.
"There's a three alarm fire way out in South Geoppolis."
"Follow me," said Katy.

So Katy plowed out the roads to the fire in
South Geoppolis.

On the way back a plane signalled for help.
The airport was snowed in.
Katy was beginning to get a little tired
but she wouldn't stop . . . .
not Katy.

She hurried over to the airport
and plowed out the runways
so the airplane could land safely.

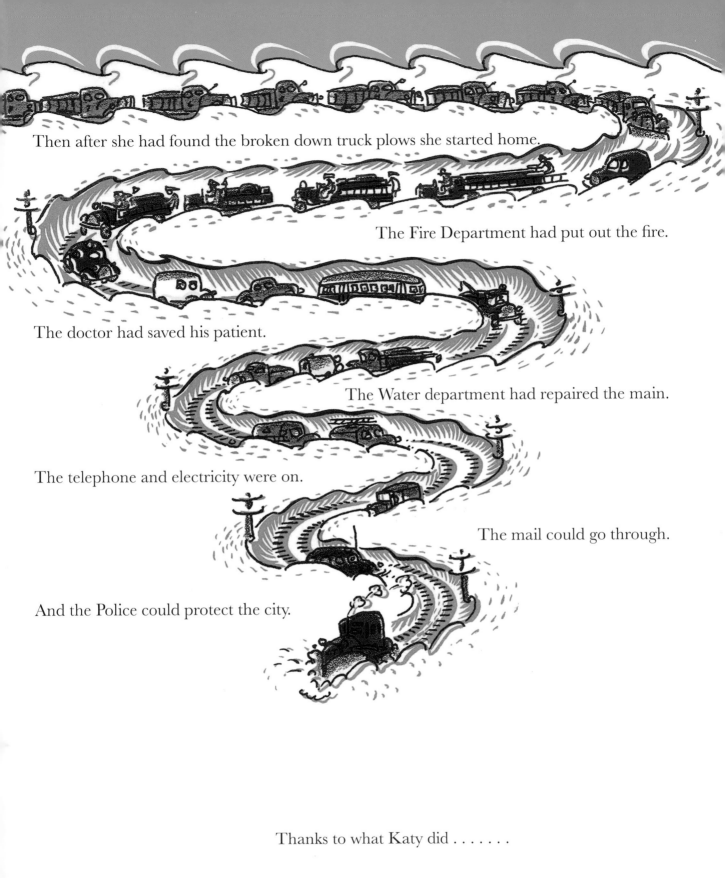

Then after she had found the broken down truck plows she started home.

The Fire Department had put out the fire.

The doctor had saved his patient.

The Water department had repaired the main.

The telephone and electricity were on.

The mail could go through.

And the Police could protect the city.

Thanks to what Katy did . . . .

Katy finished up the side streets
so traffic could move in and out and around the city.
Then she went home to rest.
Then . . . . . and only then did Katy stop.

ABOUT THE AUTHORS AND ILLUSTRATORS

H. A. REY and **MARGRET REY** escaped Nazi-occupied Paris in 1940 by bicycle, carrying the manuscript for the first book about Curious George. They came to live in the United States, and *Curious George* was published in 1941. You can learn more about the Reys and Curious George and access games, activities, and more at www.curiousgeorge.com.

The author and illustrator **NANCY COFFELT** loves dogs, and pugs are some of her favorites! She and her two dogs meet up with them on walks and in the park and, yes, have even seen them traveling down the highway in big rigs. She lives in Portland, Oregon.

DEB LUND is a dino-fabulous picture book writer. Deb is also a teacher, singer, unicycle rider, and mom to her three kids. She lives on an island in Washington. www.deblund.com

HOWARD FINE is an award-winning illustrator of many popular picture books, including the best-selling *Piggie Pie!* by Margie Palatini. Howard makes people smile with his books and in his other role as a dentist. He lives near New York City. www.howardfineillustration.com

LISA WHEELER is the author of several award-winning picture books, including *Sixteen Cows* and *Mammoths on the Move,* which received a Parent's Choice Recommended award. She lives near Jackson, Michigan. www.lisawheelerbooks.com

IVAN BATES is the well-known illustrator of Lisa Wheeler's *One Dark Night* and *Where, Oh Where, Is Santa Claus?*, as well as *Just You and Me, There, There,* and *The Dark at the Top of the Stairs,* by Sam McBratney. He lives in England.

MARK TODD teaches classes in publishing and children's books at Art Center College of Design in Pasadena, California. He lives and works in the Los Angeles area with his wife, artist Esther Pearl Watson, their daughter, Lili, and Mr. Pickles, a lovely French bulldog. www.marktoddillustration.com

NANCY SHAW came up with the idea for the first sheep book during a boring car trip with her husband and two children. She lives in Ann Arbor, Michigan, with her husband. www.nancyshawbooks.com

MARGOT APPLE has illustrated close to sixty books for children. *Blanket* and *Brave Martha,* which she wrote as well as illustrated, are her favorites. Her work has also been used in *Country Journal, Horticulture, Ladybug,* and *Babybug.* Margot lives near Shelburne Falls, Massachusetts, with her husband, horses, and cats.

CHRISTINE LOOMIS is the author of *The Hippo Hop* and *One Cow Coughs: A Counting Book for the Sick and Miserable.* Christine is also a longtime travel writer. She lives in San Rafael, California.

MARI TAKABAYASHI was born in Tokyo, Japan, and studied at Otsuma Women's College. She lives in Brooklyn, New York. www.maritakabayashi.com

LEDA SCHUBERT lives in north-central Vermont with her husband, Bob, and their extraordinary dogs. She is on the faculty of Vermont College of Fine Arts MFA in Writing for Children. The real Darrell dug her basement and a frog pond with his backhoe, plowed the driveway with his snowplow, and delivered firewood with his dump truck. www.ledaschubert.com.

The Caldecott medalist **MARY AZARIAN** is a gardener and a skilled woodblock artist. She received the 1999 Caldecott Medal for *Snowflake Bentley,* written by Jacqueline Briggs Martin. She lives in Vermont.

ROBERT NEUBECKER's first book for children, *Wow! City!,* won an ALA Notable Book award for 2005. A growing list of books have followed, including *Wow! Ocean!, Linus the Vegetarian T.Rex, Winter is for Snow,* and *I Got Two Dogs* by John Lithgow. www.neubeckerbooks.com

VIRGINIA LEE BURTON was the talented author and illustrator of some of the most enduring books ever written for children, including *The Little House,* winner of the 1942 Caldecott Medal. She lived with her two sons, Aristides and Michael, and her husband, George Demetrios, a sculptor, in a section of Gloucester, Massachusetts, called Folly Cove. The design class she taught there evolved into the Folly Cove Designers, a group of internationally known professional artisans.

ALICE SCHERTLE is the author of *Little Blue Truck, Little Blue Truck Leads the Way,* and many other well-loved books for children, including *Very Hairy Bear* and *All You Need for a Snowman.* She lives in Plainfield, Massachusetts.

JILL McELMURRY is the illustrator of *Little Blue Truck* and *Little Blue Truck Leads the Way* by Alice Schertle, as well as her own *Mad About Plaid* and *I'm Not a Baby!.* She lives in Albuquerque, New Mexico.